Mangoes
&
Bananas

Deep in the Indonesian rainforest lived Kanchil, the mouse deer. His best friend was Monyet, the monkey.

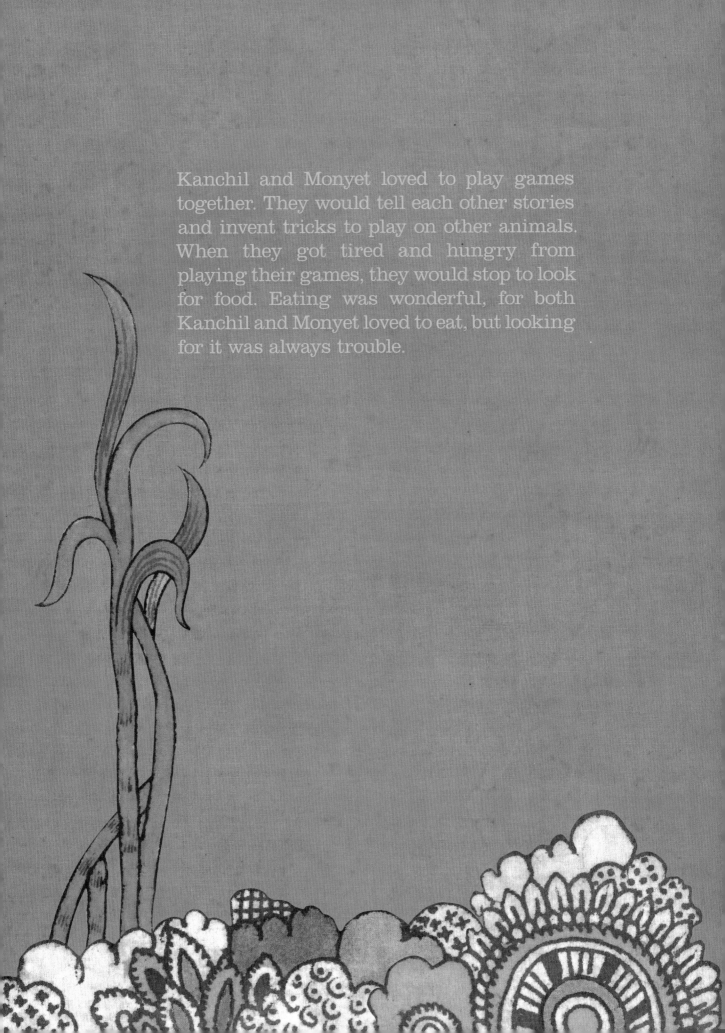

Kanchil and Monyet loved to play games together. They would tell each other stories and invent tricks to play on other animals. When they got tired and hungry from playing their games, they would stop to look for food. Eating was wonderful, for both Kanchil and Monyet loved to eat, but looking for it was always trouble.

One day, Kanchil and Monyet were playing together, when Kanchil suddenly stopped.

'Monyet, I'm hungry!' Kanchil complained. 'Do you know how to get food without looking for it?'

'Carry lots of food around with us?' asked Monyet. 'That would get tiring!'

'No, Monyet. I have an idea. Let's plant a garden. Like the humans do.'

'Our own garden? But what would we plant?'

Kanchil knew what he wanted to plant, and he also knew what Monyet would want to plant.

He said, 'Guess what I want to plant? I'll give you a clue: it has a big seed.'

Monyet scratched his head and thought a while.

'I don't know. A coconut? Sugar-coated lemons?'

'No, silly, mangoes! Mangoes are my favourite fruit. I want to plant a mango tree in our garden.'

'What a good idea!' said Monyet, but he still thought sugar-coated lemons would be better. 'Now, you guess what I want to plant in our garden. It's my favourite fruit.'

'Let's see...' said Kanchil, pretending to think hard. 'I think you want to plant... bananas!'

Monyet jumped up and down. 'That's right!'

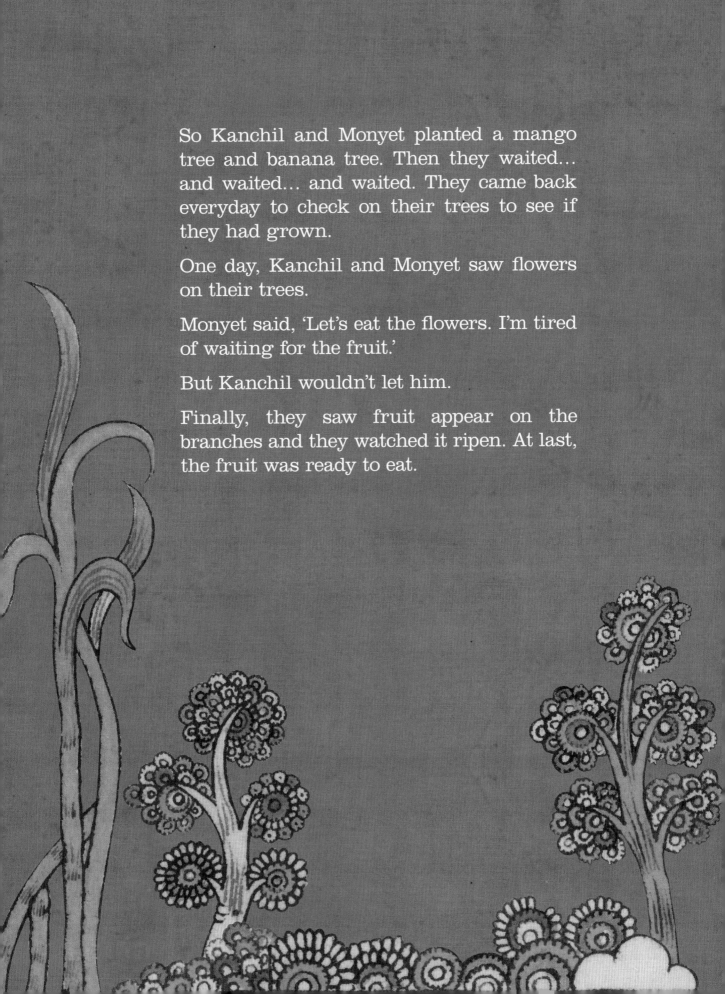

So Kanchil and Monyet planted a mango tree and banana tree. Then they waited... and waited... and waited. They came back everyday to check on their trees to see if they had grown.

One day, Kanchil and Monyet saw flowers on their trees.

Monyet said, 'Let's eat the flowers. I'm tired of waiting for the fruit.'

But Kanchil wouldn't let him.

Finally, they saw fruit appear on the branches and they watched it ripen. At last, the fruit was ready to eat.

Kanchil and Monyet brought a basket each
to carry their bananas and mangoes.

They stood under their trees, looking up
and admiring their fruit.

Then Kanchil suddenly realized something. How could he not have thought of it before?

Kanchil had forgotten that he couldn't climb trees!

How was he to get his mangoes down?

Kanchil said, 'Monyet, you know how to climb trees. So why don't you pick the fruit? Then we'll share it, half for you, half for me.'

'Fine,' said Monyet and scampered up the banana tree. He climbed right to the top.

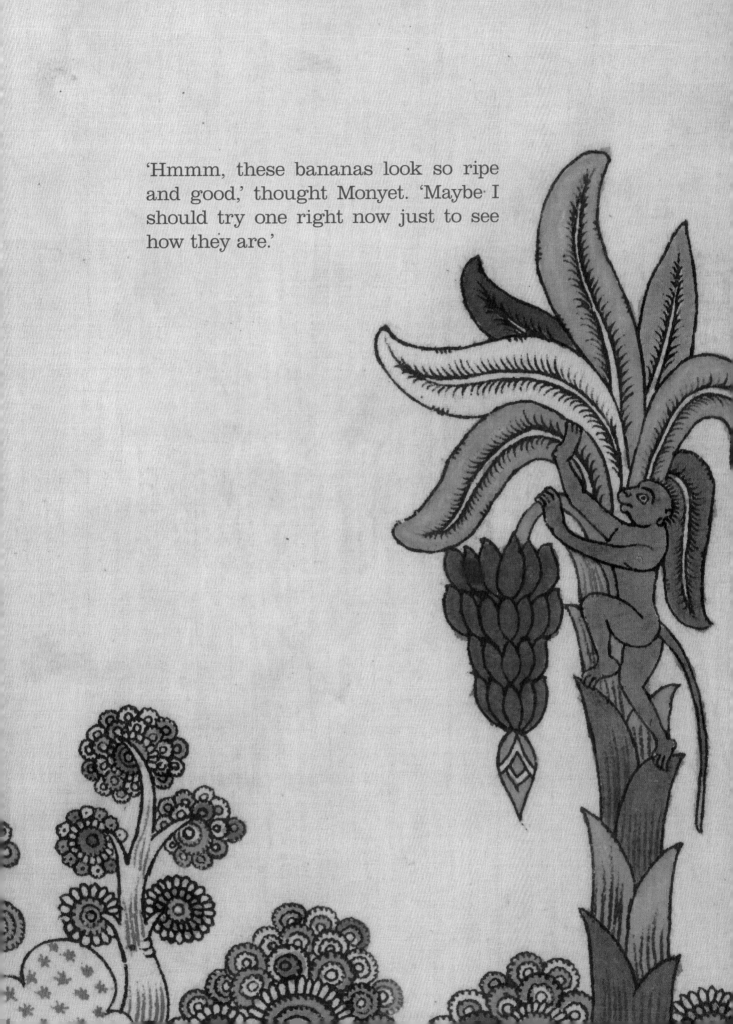

'Hmmm, these bananas look so ripe and good,' thought Monyet. 'Maybe I should try one right now just to see how they are.'

He made sure Kanchil wasn't looking and ate one banana. It tasted as good as it looked! So he ate another... and another... and another.

'Hey Monyet! Don't eat all of the bananas! Remember to bring some down for me!' Kanchil shouted.

But Monyet was eating the bananas as fast as he could. They were so good that he couldn't stop himself.

Soon all the bananas in the tree were gone. Monyet knew he had done an awful thing. He slowly climbed down with the empty basket.

'I'm sorry,' said Monyet. 'But the bananas were so good, I couldn't help eating them all myself.'

Kanchil was very upset. But he was glad that Monyet had climbed the banana tree first, instead of the mango tree. Now he would be too full to eat any of Kanchil's mangoes.

'Well, Monyet,' said Kanchil. 'That was not fair of you. You agreed that half of the bananas would be for me, but you ate them all. That means all the mangoes are mine. Now bring them down for me. And don't eat any of them!'

Monyet slowly started up the mango tree.

He slowly plucked a few mangoes and put them in the basket. How ripe and juicy and delicious they looked!

Monyet felt his appetite start to come back. But he had promised to bring all the fruits down for Kanchil. He looked at a mango, then down at Kanchil, and then back at the mango.

'Kanchil wouldn't miss just one mango, would he?' he thought. And the mango disappeared into his mouth.

'Kanchil wouldn't miss just one more,' he said to himself and reached for another mango.

Kanchil saw what was happening. Monyet had eaten all the bananas and now he was eating his mangoes as well! He had to find a way of stopping him.

Then Kanchil had a great idea.

'Monyet!' he shouted. 'You've got a face like a papaya!'

Monyet paused with a mango in his hand. 'What did Kanchil say?' he thought.

'And not only that. Your nose looks like a carrot!' Kanchil shouted from down below. 'And your head looks like a cabbage.'

Monyet was really shocked. 'How dare he say that my head looks like a cabbage!' he thought.

'And not only that. Your ears look like radishes!'

This was too much. Monyet thought his ears were the finest in all the forest. He shouted down to Kanchil. 'That's not nice! Stop saying those things!'

But Kanchil kept on.

'Monyet smells like an onion. Monyet's hair looks like string beans. Monyet's face looks like an eggplant!'

Monyet looked around for something to throw at Kanchil to get him to stop. He grabbed a mango.

'This will teach you!' Monyet shouted and threw the mango down at Kanchil.

Kanchil darted out of the way, shouting, 'Ha, ha, you missed me! Your face is as red as a tomato!'

Monyet took careful aim and threw another mango at Kanchil. And another... and another... and another...

Finally Monyet reached for the last mango
on the tree, took aim, and threw it as hard
he could at Kanchil.

'This will teach you to make fun of me!' shouted Monyet.

And with that Kanchil ran off into the forest with his mangoes, leaving Monyet still up in the mango tree.

His clever plan had worked!

Kalamkari
Ancient Indian Textile Art

The illustrations in this book were created in the traditional Indian art form of Kalamkari. 'Kalam-kari', literally meaning 'Pen-manship', developed on the southeastern coast of India in the 17ᵗʰ century. Originally, Kalamkari art illustrated the Indian epics on large pieces of textile, which were hung in temples and carried from town to town by minstrels.

The intricacy and beauty of Kalamkari fabrics, with their hand-painted designs using natural dyes, led to a textile trade with England, France, Holland, Persia and Indonesia. European merchants not only bought and sold Kalamkari cloth, they also studied its manufacturing process in order to develop their own form of printed cloth, called calico. Calico was made in European factories and then shipped to India where it sold for much less than the original handmade fabric. In an effort to compete with European cloth, calico factories were then built in India, and the handmade process began to fade. Kalamkari in the original way began to be revived once again in independent India, when textile co-operatives were formed and began using the old methods.

This is the first time that Kalamkari art has been used to illustrate a book. The combination of story and art recalls an earlier historical encounter - when handpainted textiles first made their way from India to Indonesia, during the early days of colonial trade on the high seas.

Each image in this book was created following the traditional process:

Preparing the Cloth

Cotton fabric is first washed and then treated with cowdung. It is then soaked in a mixture of myrobalan, a fruit containing tannin, and cow's milk. The myrobalan allows the dye to bind to the cloth and the milk keeps it from running. The cloth is then dried in the sun and turns light yellow in colour.

Sketching

The images and designs are sketched on to the cloth with a burnt twig. A mixture of iron rust shavings and palm jaggery is then soaked for 15 days. This solution is used to darken the outlines of each drawing. The ink is applied using a sharpened bamboo stick wound with thread. The thread absorbs and dispenses the ink as the artist works.

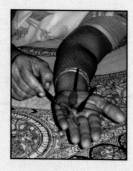

Colouring

All colours that appear on Kalamkari cloth are produced in three rounds of vegetable dye: red, yellow and blue, always applied in that order. Each round is done separately and the cloth is washed and re-prepared each time.

Washing

Before each dye is applied, the cloth is painted with an alum solution only on the areas meant to be red. This alum acts as a mordant, or a substance that fixes natural dye on material. After 24 hours, excess mordant is removed by washing the cloth in water.

Boiling & Drying

The cloth is boiled with the red dye and then moved to a vat of water with dissolved cowdung to clean the areas of the cloth where the dye has bled. The cloth is set out to dry in the sun and is then dipped in cow's milk to prevent the dye from spreading.

Final Product

This same process is repeated for the yellow and blue dyes. After all dye is on, the cloth is fixed and you have the final product.

All photographs taken at Kalakshetra Kalamkari Unit, Chennai, India

Mangoes and Bananas
Copyright ©2006

For the text: Nathan Scott Kumar
For the illustrations: T. Balaji

For this edition:
Tara Publishing Ltd., UK <www.tarabooks.com/uk>
and
Tara Publishing, India <www.tarabooks.com>

Design: Natasha Chandani, www.localfarang.com
Production: C. Arumugam
Kalamkari Documentation: Lisa Gaynon and Nicole Gurgel

Printed in Thailand by Sirivatana Interprint PCL.

We would like to thank Kalakshetra Kalamkari Unit - Chennai, India
for their assistance with this project.

ISBN: 81-86211-06-3

CHILDREN'S BOOKS FROM TARA PUBLISHING

As children's books the world over become increasingly homogenous, we dare to offer completely fresh approaches. Internationally recognised for its innovation, Tara's list features a number of prize-winning titles. Merging strong concepts with playful language, illustration and design, these challenging books offer children unexpected worlds to delight in.

EXCUSE ME, IS THIS INDIA?

Illustrated with exquisite Indian cloth by the well known Swiss textile artist Anita Leutwiler, this is a story of travel through a child's imagination. The brilliant nonsense verse from Anushka Ravishankar captures the surreal mixture of places, people and creatures that make up India.

Ravishankar/Leutwiler
Age: 8+
ISBN: 81-86211-56-X

HENSPARROW TURNS PURPLE

Designed as a scroll, it also makes a long wall picture. This cheerful adaptation of a folk tale tells the story of Hen-sparrow, who falls into a vat of dye, and turns quite purple. The illustrations recall the exquisite art of Indian miniature painting. Hand printed on handmade paper.

❊ **Award Winner**

Wolf/Biswas
Age: 4+
ISBN: 81-86211-19-5

THE VERY HUNGRY LION

The Very Hungry Lion is an adaptation of a traditional folk tale about a lazy lion who would rather trick other animals than hunt for his food. The vibrant and humorous art is rendered in the Warli style of folk painting from western India, usually painted with white chalk on the mud walls of tribal houses. Hand-printed on handmade paper.

❊ **Award Winner**

Wolf/Roy
Age: 4+
ISBN: 81-86211-02-0

ONE, TWO, TREE!

This stunning number book for young children features art by Durga Bai, a woman tribal artist from the Gond tradition of central India. The absurdly charming tale leads children to hunt for the improbable number of animals who clamber aboard an ever-expanding tree, introducing even very young children to exceptional art.

❊ **Award Winner**

Ravishankar/Rao/Bai
Age: 4+
ISBN: 81-86211-80-2

FOR A COMPLETE CATALOGUE VISIT WWW.TARABOOKS.COM

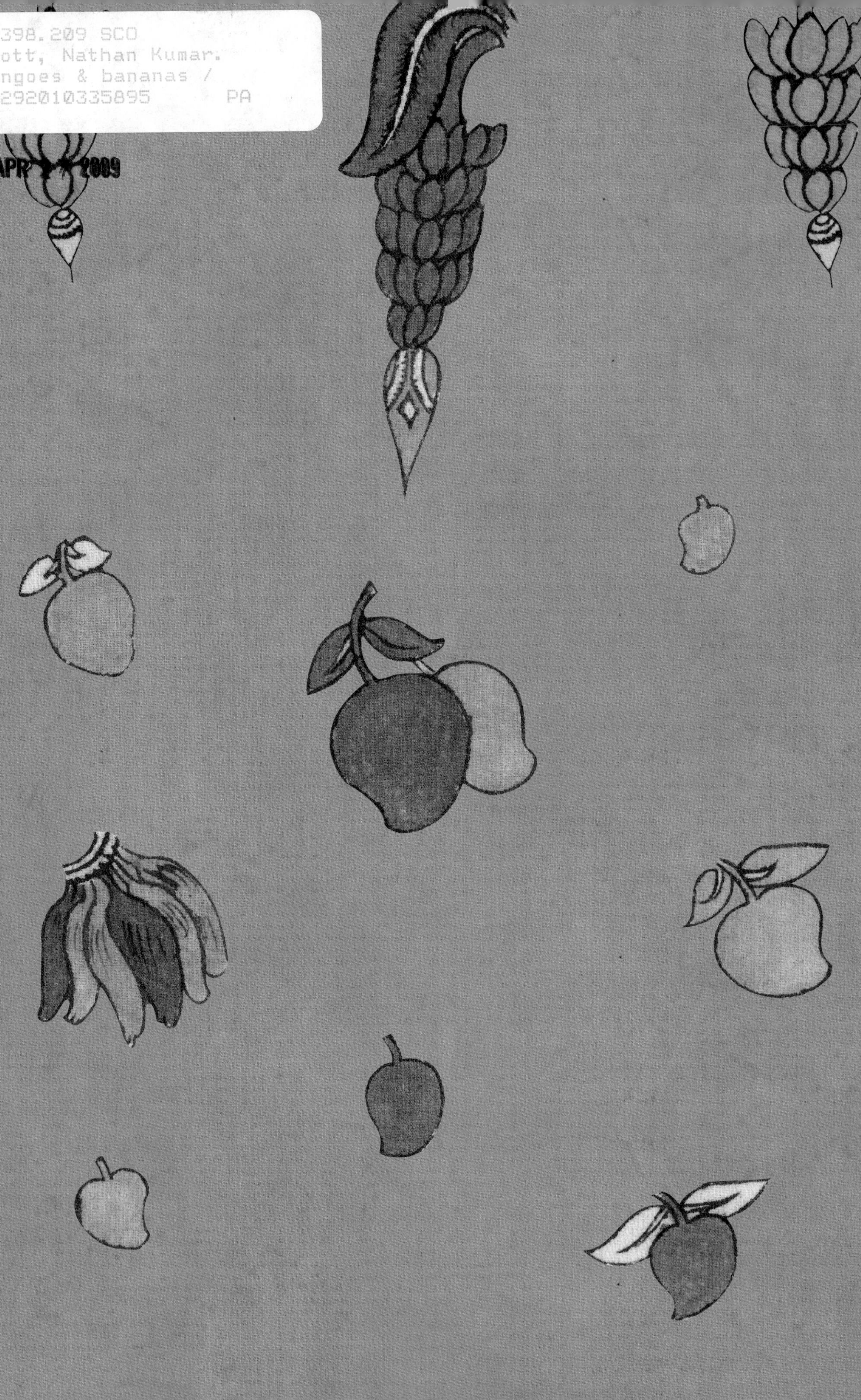